SOME FROG!

Eve Bunting

SOME FROG!

Illustrated by Scott Medlock

VOYAGER BOOKS · HARCOURT, INC.

San Diego   New York   London

With special thanks to
Mrs. Jackie Kitchen and her class.
—E. B.

www.harcourt.com

First Voyager Books edition 2002
Voyager Books is a trademark of Harcourt, Inc., registered in
the United States of America and/or other jurisdictions.

The Library of Congress has cataloged the hardcover edition as follows:
Bunting, Eve, 1928–
Some frog!/Eve Bunting; illustrated by Scott Medlock.
p. cm.
Summary: Billy is disappointed when his father doesn't show up to help him
catch a frog for the frog-jumping competition at school, but the one he and his mother
catch wins the championship and Billy begins to accept his father's absence.
[1. Fathers and sons—Fiction. 2. Frogs—Fiction. 3. Divorce—Fiction.
4. Contests—Fiction.] I. Medlock, Scott, ill. II. Title.
PZ7.B91527Slk 1998
[Fic]—dc20 96-24844
ISBN 0-15-277082-8
ISBN 0-15-216384-0 pb

TWP 12 11 10 9 8
4500329016

The illustrations in this book were done in oils on paper.
The display type was set in Heatwave.
The text type was set in Palatino.
Color separations by United Graphic Pte. Ltd., Singapore
Printed and bound by Tien Wah Press, Singapore
Production supervision by Sandra Grebenar and Wendi Taylor
Designed by Camilla Filancia

For frogs everywhere
—E. B.

For Diane D'Andrade,
with special thanks
for helping me
leapfrog into illustrating
children's books
—S. M.

Chapter 1

Tomorrow our class is having a frog-jumping competition. The winner gets two tickets to a Cubs game. If I win, I'll take my dad.

Dad says our meadow creek has no frogs in it, just crawdaddies, so tonight at seven he's coming to our house and we're going to Miller's Pond to get me a frog. Dad says it's so shallow we can wade right in. Frogs come out at night and we'll be there waiting for them.

Grandpa has a plastic bucket all ready. His big waders are standing by the door for Dad to take.

"Billy, you use my super flashlight," Grandpa tells me. "I put in new batteries, so it's good and strong. You can stun a frog out of his head with a sharp light in his eyes."

I nod. My grandpa knows a lot.

"I'd go with you," he says, "if it weren't for these crock legs of mine." Grandpa has arthritis really bad. "I can find frogs in places they don't even know they're at," he says.

I always like Grandpa to come on outings with me, but tonight it's going to be just me and Dad. It's going to be so great.

We have supper as soon as Mom comes home from work. She's going to make frog cookies for the after-jump party tomorrow. Grandma has made me a frog suit from stiff green paper. We have to come dressed as someone, or something, for the party, and Grandma says I might just as well be a frog.

I stand by the window to wait for Dad's truck.

But it doesn't come.

And it doesn't come.

Mom goes in her bedroom. I know she's making a phone call because I hear the little *peep* as she pushes the talk button. I don't hear her say anything, though.

When she comes back Grandma raises her eyebrows and Mom shakes her head. They think I don't see, but I do. Mom called Dad and he's not home. That could be bad, but it could be good. Maybe he's on his way.

Chapter 2

Mom asks if I want to help make the cookies while I wait.

Grandma says she needs me to try on my frog suit again.

Grandpa has painted a frog mask for me to wear.

"Can you see? Can you breathe?" Grandma asks.

I nod, though it's hard.

"You look very froggy," Grandma says.

"Very amphibian," Grandpa adds, and winks. "*Amphibian*'s just a fancy name for a frog. Let's hear you croak, Billy."

My croak isn't great. Usually I'm a good croaker. I like the mask because it covers up my face and I think I'm starting to cry a little bit. Dad's not coming. I can't keep wearing the mask all night, though, so I take it off.

Grandpa starts telling me how he once had a frog. "It got away from me and scared your mother. She was just a little girl then."

"Mom was afraid of frogs?" I can't believe it. My mom's not scared of anything, not even Grandpa's big old mean bull, Jericho.

I can't stop looking at the clock up on the kitchen wall. Now it says 8:10.

"What time do frogs go to sleep?" I ask.

"They stay up all night," Grandpa says. "Don't worry about that. The later it gets, the tireder they are. You can catch them then, smooth as syrup. Don't worry at all."

That's not what's worrying me. And my grandpa knows me so well, he knows that, too.

Chapter 3

Mom takes the cookies out of the oven. She bangs the oven door, and Grandpa says softly, "Relax, Eileen. Just relax."

Mom slides the hot metal cookie tray onto a rack beside me. "Try one," she says.

It's 8:35. I've left the window and I'm sitting at the table pretending to read my *Ranger Rick* magazine.

I take a cookie. It's a nice grass green color. The chocolate chips inside are warm and squishy. "Good," I say. I look up at her.

"I don't think Dad's coming."

"No," she says.

"Why does he tell me he'll do things when he's not going to?" I ask.

I feel a tear starting for real, and I hold the magazine in front of my face. It's almost as good as the mask. "I don't get it," I mutter. "Are all dads like that?"

"No," Mom says. "Some dads are fine."

"Maybe he's crashed his truck," I say.

Mom touches my arm. "I don't think so."

Every time Dad doesn't come, I ask if maybe he's crashed his truck. Every single time. It's so stupid. I sound like a stupid baby.

Mom takes her parka and my jacket off the hooks. She tosses the jacket to me. "Here, put this on," she says. "It's going to be cold at Miller's Pond."

"Dad," she orders, "give me the flashlight. Billy, you bring the bucket."

"We're still going?" I ask.

"Of course we're still going," Mom says. "What do you think? We're going to get us a jumper."

Chapter 4

Miller's Pond is as black as Pennzoil, except where the moon floats yellow on top. Bulrushes spike its edges. A million crickets sing their little hearts out. Mom has Grandpa's big waders on, and my jeans are tucked into my rubber boots.

"Shine the flashlight," I tell her. "Grandpa says you can stun a frog out of his head with a sharp light in his eyes."

Mom sweeps the beam over the water. It looks like a smaller, moving moon. "See any frogs?" she whispers.

"Uh-uh." But I know they're here. There must be a million crickets, and we don't see them, either.

Mom goes in the pond first. "Wow, it's cold," she whispers. "I can feel it through the waders."

The crickets shut up. They must have a secret
signal, because they all stop at once, listening.
The only sound is the whispering of the bulrushes.
Or the whispering of the frogs in the bulrushes.

"Come on, Billy Boy," Mom urges.

We walk slowly, trying not to splash. We don't talk.

I know the frogs are listening. I walk through the yellow ball of moon, breaking it in pieces.

I think I see a frog, but when I get there he has vanished. Frogs are fast. I wonder if Dad would have found us one by now. I bet he would.

Once I think I hear him call to me from the bank. My heart leaps with excitement. He came! He was just late, that's all.

But it's a night bird, an owl maybe, that calls in the branches. Just a night bird.

Chapter 5

"Look!" Mom points the light and I see a frog.

He's huge.

He's gigantic.

He's a monster. His throat bulges in and out. He's covered with bumps. His eyes are as big as marbles.

"Get him, Billy!" Mom is so excited she's shining the flashlight straight into the sky.

I puddle hard through the water, but I'm trailing the bucket and it gets water in it and slows me down. I grab for the frog and he jumps. He jumps clear across Miller's Pond.

"Gee jeepers," I breathe. "Did you see that? Did you see how far he jumped?"

Then there's a mammoth splash.

Mom has thrown herself flat across the water like a swimmer starting a race. She disappears. The pond-moon is shaking.

"Mom!" I yell. I can't see well because she has dropped the flashlight. Then the dark shape of her head pops up.

"I've got him! I've got him!" she yells. "Bring the bucket. He's slipping. He's getting away. Quick, Billy."

I'm so quick.

I splash and kick and I'm right next to her. She's holding the frog in both hands, and her hands are moving like she's climbing a rope. He's wriggling and she's doing her best to hold on to him.

I empty the water out of the bucket and she slides him in.

"Got him," she says. I hear her grin. "We've got us our frog!"

Chapter 6

We walk sideways. I'm carrying the bucket and we spread our hands across the top so our frog can't jump out. I feel him leaping against my splayed-out fingers, cold and wet and slippery.

"That's some frog we caught there," Mom says, all happy.

"Yeah!" I'm happy, too.

We find the piece of thin wood we left at the side of the pond. The bucket's top is round and the wood isn't, so there are air places. They're not big, though, so the frog can't squirm free.

Mom and I shake hands. She's dripping pond water, and I'm as wet as if I'd taken the dive myself.

"I've got to go back for Grandpa's flashlight," she says, and splashes away again.

While she's gone I talk to my frog. "Don't worry," I say. "Tomorrow night we'll bring you back here. It'll be a vacation for you. Honest. And you'll have fun. It'll be like going to the frog Olympics."

Mom's back. She has the flashlight, but when she presses the switch it doesn't work. "Wet batteries," she says. "It was for a good cause."

"The frog's name's Amphibian," I say.

"Great. Keep the bucket covered. We don't want Amphibian to use up his strength jumping around in the car." She taps the bucket. "Save it all for tomorrow, Amphibian."

"He looked like a pretty good jumper," I tell Mom.

"He looked like a winner to me," Mom says.

We're shaking and shivering with cold. Mom finds a blanket on the backseat and wraps it around me. "Hot showers," she says. "Hot showers for both of us. Amphibian is excused."

"Maybe Dad will be at the house when we get back," I say. "Maybe we can show him Amphibian."

"Maybe," Mom says.

Chapter 7

Dad isn't there when we get home.
"Did he call?" I ask.

"No." Grandma is angry. I can tell because her mouth is all puckered up as if she wants a kiss. But it's not that. "Likely he forgot, same as always," she says.

"Sh, Mom," my mom says.

Grandpa has been busy. He's been to our meadow creek in spite of his bum leg. He holds up a jar of water bugs. "A champion amphibian's got to eat," he says.

He drops a couple of bugs into the bucket.

I close my eyes. I know a champion has to eat. But I don't have to watch.

The jumping competition is tomorrow at three.

Mom says she'll try to get away from work early for at least part of the competition, and for the party.

"We'll not miss a minute of anything," Grandpa tells me.

"And we'll bring your frog suit," Grandma says.

Mom lets me have Amphibian sleep in his bucket by my bed. But he's pretty noisy jumping around in there. So we end up putting him in the bathroom.

Grandpa comes in my room later.

"Are you asleep?" he whispers.

"No, I'm too excited," I say.

He sits on my chair on top of tomorrow's clean clothes and leans his cane against my bed. "Here are a few tips from my frog-jumping expertise," he says.

"First, stroke his back legs gently. Gently gets results.

"Second, whisper in his ear that you expect him to

win. Like it's a secret bargain between the two of you."

"Frogs have ears?" I ask.

Grandpa pats his own ears. "They have to be there someplace.

"And third and most important, promise him a Fig Newton when he wins."

"Frogs like Fig Newtons?" I ask, astonished. "I didn't know that."

Grandpa stands up. "Is there any creature alive on planet Earth that doesn't like a Fig Newton? Get real, boy."

"True," I say.

"What if I win?" I ask. "It'll be so great. But what if I don't?"

"One thing's for sure. It'll be one way or the other," Grandpa tells me.

I nod. I'm wondering if Dad will be at the competition, but I don't ask. I know what Grandpa will say. "Maybe."

That's what you say when you're pretty sure it's not going to happen.

Chapter 8

The next day I take Amphibian to school in his bucket. I've peeked at him and he's looking good.

"The night's rest and the water bugs will make him feisty," Grandpa said after breakfast. "He'll jump over the moon."

"But it's daytime," I reminded him.

"Over the school, then," Grandpa said.

At school Mrs. Cooper gives us numbers to put on our buckets. Then we line up the buckets under the windows. The frogs inside croak and clatter and make little peeping noises. The buckets slide around. We keep getting up to check on our frogs and to put the lids on better.

Todd Junwon's frog gets out and he chases it around the room, calling, "Bop Belcher, Bop Belcher," and snapping his fingers as if he's calling a dog.

"Heel, Bop Belcher," Pauline Kaminski says. We're all laughing so hard we're falling out of our desks.

Our teacher keeps saying, "Get him, Todd. Get him."

Finally Todd corners Bop Belcher by her desk.

Amphibian is Number 7.

Sylvia Lopez says that's a lucky number.

I've checked on everybody's frogs. Amphibian's the biggest.

Debbie Jackson's is the next biggest. His name is Grover.

"My dad caught four," she says. "We let three go."

"My mom caught Amphibian," I say.

"Don't you have a dad?" Debbie asks.

"Sure I do. Everybody has a dad. I think. My mom and dad split up, so mine doesn't live with us, that's all. I have a grandpa and grandma, though. And my mom."

"I don't have a grandpa," Debbie says.

I feel sorry for her. Not having a grandpa is sad.

We are all very hyper waiting for three o'clock.

"Hyper down, students," Mrs. Cooper orders.

We can't.

She reads us a story about Huckleberry Finn and his friend Tom Sawyer. They had a frog-jumping competition, too.

We have a mock frog-jump contest in the classroom using paper clips and cotton balls. Mrs. Cooper makes us measure all the distances. The longest fake jump is five feet, and that is not mine. Five feet equals sixty inches. Mrs. Cooper never misses a teaching opportunity. Mine is just three feet three inches, or thirty-nine inches.

I sincerely hope my frog jumps better than my cotton ball.

Chapter 9

Three o'clock comes at last.

As soon as the bell rings we grab our buckets and hurry to the playground.

I eyeball the parking lot. Dad's truck is yellow, and he has a big fake daisy on the radio antenna. It's easy to spot. It isn't there. But I see Grandpa's blue Chevrolet. Heavenly blue he calls it. More like blue mold, Grandma says. I know Mom won't be here for a while, maybe not even till party time.

There are lots of parents in the playground already. Lots of dads.

Grandma and Grandpa wave to me.

Justin Pepper's frog, Gorf, is Number 1.

It's pretty funny, because Gorf won't jump. But it's pretty embarrassing, too. I hope that doesn't happen to me with Amphibian.

"Go!" Justin yells. "Jump, Gorf." Justin's face is red. I can see he's making a lot of mistakes. He's not whispering anything in Gorf's ear, and he's definitely not stroking Gorf's back legs. His dad's shouting advice, but it's bad advice. I can tell Justin's dad isn't an expert like Grandpa.

Finally Gorf jumps. Three feet, or thirty-six inches. Then he takes off. He crosses the school yard in three monstrous jumps. I swear each one is twenty feet.

Justin is as mad as a wet crow because Mrs. Cooper says only the official jump counts.

Jennifer Ryan is second. Her frog is Lars. He's named after the drummer in her favorite rock band. He's a pretty ugly old frog, but he can jump like crazy.

"Ten feet three inches," Mrs. Cooper calls out.

We are impressed. Everyone whoops and hollers.

Lars looks stunned as Jennifer picks him up. He looks dead, in fact. But he isn't. It's more like he's in a trance. Maybe cheering has the same effect on a frog as a sharp light in his eyes.

I'm all the time checking to see if Dad has come. Pauline Kaminski told me the *Morning Gazette* had an announcement about the contest. She said it gave the time and place and everything. I guess Dad just didn't see it.

When it's Amphibian's turn, I carry him to the starting line. My hands are sweating, and what with my sweat and his natural slipperiness I have to be really careful.

"Billy!" someone calls. I look up and it's Mom.

She's waving like mad. I can't wave back of course, but I'm really happy she made it in time.

I crouch down. Amphibian's quivering. He smells like Miller's Pond. His throat bulges and wilts, bulges and wilts.

I whisper all the secret stuff in his ear, then let him go and gently stroke his back legs.

Amphibian jumps.

Chapter 10

Amphibian flies through the air.
He's a bird!
He's a plane!
He's a superfrog!

We are awed into silence.

Amphibian sits, still as a frog statue. It's as if he's done his thing and he knows it.

I run and pick him up and whisper in his ear. "You are *wonderful*."

"Fifteen feet two inches," Mrs. Cooper calls. She's so awed herself she doesn't ask us to turn it into inches. A good thing. We'd need a calculator for that one.

Of course, there are nineteen more contestants. I stand beside Amphibian's bucket and watch. I report the length of each jump to him. Normally I'm not a nail-biter, but today I'm biting.

No jump comes close. Not one. We are declared the winners.

I'd hug Amphibian if I could, but I know he wouldn't like it. I wouldn't like it much, either.

Mom and Grandma and Grandpa are hopping up and down as I walk up to get my prize. Two tickets. The Cubs versus the Dodgers next Saturday night. It's the game of the season.

"They're running a bus from town to Wrigley Field,"

Mrs. Cooper says. "We've got two bus tickets for you, too."

Grandpa produces something from his pocket and slides it into Amphibian's bucket.

"The Fig Newton," he whispers to me. "A promise is a promise."

I hate the thought that pops into my head. *Except for Dad.* I squeeze the thought out again before it spoils the day.

We all go back to the classroom and dress up for the party. In my opinion my frog suit is the best. The mask is a masterpiece.

The parents have made great frog stuff.

There are Mom's frog cookies; frog eggs, which are spoonfuls of green Jell-O in paper cups; tiny tadpoles, which are chocolate kisses; and frog lips. They are really cut-up licorice strings.

"Do frogs have lips?" Debbie Jackson asks me.

"Do chickens?" I ask her.

One of the parents has brought swamp water, which is green Kool-Aid.

Grandpa downs a cup of it and says, "I like Grandma's green Kool-Aid better. She puts fresh mint in hers."

"Oh, shush!" Grandma is really pleased.

Grandpa has another cup. "The mint would enhance it," he says. "But it's really good the way it is."

That night Mom and I take Amphibian back home.

Miller's Pond is still dark as Pennzoil. The moon floats yellow on the water. The crickets chirp their hearts out.

I lift Amphibian and Mom shines the flashlight into the bucket. The Fig Newton's still there.

"We won't tell Grandpa," she says. She sinks the cookie in the pond. "Some other frog will be mad for it."

I lean down and put Amphibian in a gap in the bulrushes. He jumps once and he's in the water. Another jump and he's gone.

"Thanks," I call. "So long, Amphibian."

"It was a great day," I tell Mom. "The best of my life so far."

"Good." Her voice is soft. "You didn't miss your dad too much?"

  "I missed him," I say. "I'll always miss him, but . . ."
I stop. "It's like Grandpa said about the Kool-Aid.
Having Dad there would have enhanced everything,
but it's really very good the way it is."

  A little wind rustles the bulrushes. The cattails
sway. I can smell the pond.

"Want to see the Cubs beat the Dodgers next Saturday night?" I ask.

Mom moves so her shoulder touches mine. "Is that a date?" she asks.

"Sure is."

We swing hands, and I think, next year if there's a frog-jumping competition, we'll come back here and find Amphibian. Maybe Dad will be with us. Maybe he'll be swinging my other hand. Maybe we'll all be together again.

Maybe, I think. Maybe.